Tim Powers

MORE WALLS BROKEN

MORE WALLS BROKEN

Tim Powers

Subterranean Press 2019

First Edition

ISBN
978-1-59606-886-5

Subterranean Press
PO Box 190106
Burton, MI 48519

subterraneanpress.com

Manufactured in the United States of America

For Bill and Peggy Wu
and Ken Estes

When the night security guard had closed the gates, the white Ford van moved slowly up the driveway, past the dark windows of the Spanish-style information center on the left, and halted a few yards short of the open-sided electric cart. The cart's headlights shone toward the gates and Newport Boulevard beyond, while the van's were pointed the other way, but it was the diffuse white radiance of the full moon that lit the wall and the asphalt lane and the trees over on the eastern edge of the cemetery.

Having re-locked the gate, the guard walked up to the driver's side window of the van, first noting the California State University logo painted on the side.

The window was down. "About an hour," said the guard, "according to the permit. Right?"

The elderly driver cleared his throat. "That should be ample," he agreed. A man seated beside him leaned across and said, "Just taking core soil samples from six locations. Well away from any graves!"

The guard squinted into the van's dim interior. "It said ground water contamination."

"The possibility thereof," said the man in the passenger seat. "Breakdown of coffin-making materials—metal, varnish, sealers. We'll be testing specifically for evidence of ammonium copper quaternary or copper boron azole. There, uh, may be some pathogenic fumes."

"Huh. Better you than me. My job to keep azoles out." The security guard was chuckling to himself as he got into the electric cart and steered it out of the way.

A cold breeze smelling of clay swept across the moonlit lawns, and the van's driver pressed the armrest button to raise the window as he drove forward. "You cover...*copper boron azoles* in Advanced Anomalies?"

The man in the passenger seat sighed. "I had the foresight to read up on our ostensible purpose."

From behind them a third man spoke up. "That was good, Dr. Blaine, what he said. Copper quaternary! Boron!"

Blaine kept his eyes on the lane and didn't reply, and the man sitting in the back leaned against the van wall and pressed his lips together. He was an assistant professor, two years along on the tenure track, and if his publication portfolio and student evaluations and "service to the university" met with the approval of the Provost three years from now, he would have tenure; if not, he would have a year to find another position somewhere. This undertaking tonight should, he hoped, count as "service to the university"—to Blaine's Consciousness Research Department, in any case—though he wished his Sociology degree had proven acceptable to a more orthodox department at the university, and he had little confidence that the three of them would actually accomplish anything here tonight. He queasily hoped not, in fact. Still, he was demonstrating cooperation and team spirit, and meant to give it his best.

Blaine glanced at the white-haired man beside him. "Where is it, Peter?"

"That lane coming up on your left. I bestirred myself to come out here this afternoon and stick a flag on his grave." Peter Ainsworth shifted around in his seat and peered into the back of the van. "Cobb," he said, "you've got what, his *gate*, is it?"

"Yes," Cobb said, "It had to be something metal, with loosely held valence electrons, and when I went to his—"

"It's a section of chain-link fence about ten feet long," Blaine interrupted. The little flag on the grass was visible in the headlights, and he drove a few yards past it, then braked to a halt and turned off the lights and the engine. "You should have seen us loading it in," he added as he levered his door open and stepped down to the asphalt. "My back is still killing me." He carefully lifted a briefcase from the van floor and held it in both hands.

A cold breeze broke up the warm air inside the van. Cobb didn't want to climb over the gate that lay behind him, so as Ainsworth got out of the van on the right side, he crawled forward between the front seats; by the time he had got his legs under himself and climbed out of the van, the other two men had shuffled around and opened the back. Cobb followed, wishing he'd worn a sweater.

Ainsworth was impatient, and had already taken hold of one of the gate's four-foot aluminum end-poles, and even as Cobb started forward to help, the old man rocked back, tugging at it.

The chain-link gate slid halfway out of the van and then stopped, and Ainsworth let go of it and hopped awkwardly away across the moonlit asphalt.

"Christ!" he whispered, rubbing his shoulder. Cobb recalled that his health was reputedly not good. The old man glared at Cobb. "You were just supposed to get something from his house, remember? I wanted something like a doorknob."

Now that Armand Vitrielli was dead, Peter Ainsworth was Cobb's immediate supervisor in the Consciousness Research Department, and he was staring at Cobb now as if the younger man must be making fun of the evening's activity. Blaine simply stood silent on the grass a couple of yards away, clutching his briefcase.

"I was too late for anything like that," said Cobb hastily, "the house has been torn down, and the ground even looks scraped. But the chain-link fence that used to be around the property was all piled up next to some Dumpsters by the driveway, and I got this." He shook his head. "It wasn't easy."

"I can well imagine." Ainsworth pulled a handkerchief from the pocket of his sport coat and wiped his hands, then coughed and gingerly dabbed at his lips. He blinked at Cobb through bifocals. "You figure he spent a lot of time rubbing his fence?"

"Well," said Cobb defensively, keeping his voice down in the silent cemetery, "this was clearly the gate—there's two pairs of wheels bolted to one side—and obviously it wasn't motorized, so he'd have had to grip it and push it back and forth across the driveway to get his car in or out. I could still see the rutted patch where this must have been. So...yes, I figure he rubbed it a couple of times every day. And he lived there for thirty-some years! There ought to be plenty of accumulated aura signature on it."

"Couldn't you," said Ainsworth, tucking his handkerchief away, "have just sawed off the upright pole that he'd have taken hold of? Did you have to bring the whole damned gate?"

"How do we know whether he pulled it from one side, or pushed it from the other?" Cobb protested, waving toward the ungainly thing. "How do we know he grabbed one of the poles rather than hooking his fingers through the chain-link? I didn't want to take the chance of bringing a piece of it that he never actually handled."

Ainsworth pursed his lips and turned away, which Cobb took as grudging concession, and Blaine waved toward the postcard-sized white flag fluttering on the grass slope a few yards behind him.

"Can you carry it over to his grave?" Blaine asked. "By yourself?"

"Certainly!"

Cobb took hold of the horizontal pole and pulled; but the aluminum frame had snagged on something in the van, and it didn't move. He got a fresh grip and pulled harder, and with a metallic screech the thing slid most of the way out, leaving Cobb sitting on the pavement with the pole at his end of the gate across his lap. The far end of the thing was now wedged up against the van's ceiling.

"Quietly!" said Blaine, looking back. "You'll have the security guard over here!"

"Right," gritted Cobb, lifting the pole and hitching himself backward until he could fold his legs. He stood up and dragged the gate the rest of the way out of the van, and when the far end of it came free, the whole thing struck the pavement with a jingling rattle.

"Damn it!" whispered Ainsworth.

How has it come about, Cobb wondered miserably as he yanked the thing upright on its wheels and began rolling it like a battering ram toward the grass, that my academic career is predicated on this idiotic midnight physical exercise? Transmigration of souls indeed! These two old fools will almost certainly *not* succeed in raising and capturing the ghost of Armand Vitrielli...and they'll probably blame the failure on me.

Clive Cobb had moved to California when he had got the job at Cal State, leaving

Tim Powers

behind in Lafayette only an older brother who was a probably-corrupt city councilman, and a one-time fiancée who had reconsidered. He thought of himself as no longer a citizen of Louisiana and not yet fully a Californian, and this park-like cemetery, with trees but no visible monuments, was disorienting.

On the grass the gate was harder to push, and he was impressed that Dr. Vitrielli had managed to wrestle the thing across his driveway every day. The old man had lived alone, though he sometimes spoke of an estranged daughter in Orange. But he had seemed healthy, unlike these two colleagues of his, and absorbed in, almost obsessed with, his work; and Cobb wondered, not for the first time, what could have driven him to shoot himself two months ago.

Vitrielli had been as gruff and abrupt as Ainsworth during the first few months that Cobb had worked for him, but a shared interest in cooking and old movies had warmed him up, and Cobb had been invited to dinner at the old man's place a number of times, and had generally stayed late in long, amiable, drink-fueled discussions. On some Saturdays Cobb had even done repair work on Vitrielli's otherwise neglected twenty-year-old Buick.

In the last year, Vitrielli had given Cobb several research projects, and since the old man's suicide Cobb was the person most familiar with Vitrielli's theories...and the only one who knew how the device the old man had referred to as his slide rule was supposed to work.

"Here's his grave," said Ainsworth, tapping his wingtip shoe on a rectangular brass plate imbedded in the grass. "I suppose you may as well lay your, your *gate* next to it. May it prove," he added in a whisper, "to be indeed a gate!"

Cobb pushed the gate up beside where Ainsworth stood, and carefully laid it over sideways on the grass beside the grave marker. A ceramic disk with a photograph of Vitrielli's face printed on it was inset on the brass plate, and by moonlight Cobb could read the raised letters beside it:

ARMAND ANTONIO VITRIELLI, 1942-2018

NATURAL PHILOSOPHER

REST IN PEACE

Blaine had apparently read it too. "No rest, I'm afraid," he said. He spoke quietly, but the wind had shivered to a halt moments earlier, and his words were clear in the new silence.

Cobb looked down at the grave of his friend. He had a pack of Camels in his shirt pocket, but, though Vitrielli had smoked pipes and had had no objection to Cobb smoking cigarettes during his visits to the house, he was sure that these two older men would begin coughing theatrically if he were to take a rest and light one.

Blaine unzipped his briefcase and fumbled around inside it, finally pulling out a flat wooden box that Cobb had seen before.

"Well," he said, handing the box to Cobb, "go ahead. Call him up."

Cobb opened the box—freeing a fleeting, nostalgic whiff of Dunhill London Mixture pipe tobacco—and lifted the eight-inch length of polished black wood out of the velvet-lined interior, and gave the box back to Blaine.

The object consisted of three flat lengths of wood closely fitted together; the top and bottom ones were secured with narrow copper bands screwed to the ends, while the middle length could be slid back and forth between them. Tiny lenses had been inset into a row of holes in each piece, and a square flat cursor, inset with three lenses in line with the rows, was fitted across the three lengths and was likewise laterally moveable.

"You say he told you how to work it," said Ainsworth, waving toward the grave. "So work it." His bony old hands were shaking, and he pressed them together as if in prayer.

Cobb held the thing up and peered at it, tilting it one way and another. "I don't know if I can read the musical notes in this light."

"*Musical* notes?" hissed Blaine. "What the hell?"

"Cobb," said Ainsworth in a querulous tone, "if this is all just some crazy—"

"Complain to him, damn it, not me!" Cobb, said, more loudly than he had meant to. He waved at the grave as he recklessly pulled out the pack of cigarettes and dug a lighter from his pants pocket, nearly dropping Vitrielli's device. "He said—" and he paused to shake a cigarette free and light it, "—that the *words* of the old occult chants were just mnemonics, and that the real… *cleaving power* of the rituals was the *notes* the words were recited in."

He took a deep drag on the cigarette, and the coal glowed.

"You know," he went on, every syllable a puff of smoke, "like in Gregorian Chant— *dah dah dah* dah *dah, dah duh dah* duh *dah*. It's math, really—a specific sequence of compression frequencies projected in the air, in space and time, in certain directions." He shook his head, remembering Vitrielli explaining it to him over drinks in the old man's study. "In the Middle Ages the notes were written in what they called *neumes,* little square marks on a four-line scale, but he converted them to modern musical symbols and stamped them below the little lenses on this thing." He waved the unorthodox slide rule.

"Are you supposed to *sing?*" asked Blaine. He started to reach toward the device, then hesitated and dropped his hand. "And what are the lenses for?"

"There are only four notes, so it'll be kind of monotonous. But yes, sing, vocalize. And there are two polarized lenses in each aperture, and they can rotate independently." Cobb eyed the incongruous old chain-link gate on the grass, but didn't step toward it. "Dr. Vitrielli said the drawing object will resonate like a tuning fork, and cause the individual lenses to rotate."

Tim Powers

Ainsworth shook his head, but didn't speak.

"And then," Cobb went on, "you slide the middle bar until all three of the cursor lenses are clear, and you step forward, singing the note to the right of the cursor on the bottom row. After seven steps you move the cursor, and, depending on which lenses are clear then and which are opaque, you know which way to turn, at which of three angles, and what new note is indicated." He grinned mirthlessly at the two older men. "When I've walked in a closed loop, the lenses are supposed to all go dark, and it's over. After that, the drawing object is used up, a spent capacitor, inert. It either worked, or it didn't."

"Do it right the first time, then," advised Ainsworth.

Blaine coughed, but didn't complain about the cigarette. "'Cleaving power,' you said. What does that mean?"

"I don't know. Vitrielli got all mystical when he'd talk about it. Cleaving reality, I suppose, to let an entity from one side move to the other side."

"Does it *summon* the entity?" asked Blaine.

"It—" Cobb groped for a way to summarize the many ways Vitrielli had described the thing's intended function; "—it more opens a specific trap-door," he said finally, "as it were, for the entity to fall through."

Blaine seemed uneasy, and Cobb wondered if the old professor was only now—standing here over Armand Vitrielli's grave in this chilly moonlit cemetery—beginning to imagine that they might actually summon Vitrielli's ghost...and perhaps capture it.

Cobb shivered in the wind, and he found that his own doubts about the efficacy of the procedure no longer seemed so convincing. The old man had become a good friend, and it belatedly occurred to Cobb that a ghost might not be happy to be roused from what should have been the final rest. This stunt

Tim Powers

probably *won't* work, he thought, but—we shouldn't be doing this.

"How," Blaine began, then coughed again. "How," he said hoarsely, "will he appear? What will we see?"

Cobb shrugged, nervous himself now about what might happen. "I gather it could be a distortion in the air, like heat ripples, or even a faint translucent image of the way he looked, like the missing limbs that show up in Kirlian photography. He said there might be thumping sounds, adjustment between the regions. The air is likely to get cold as ambient energy is consumed, and the grass might appear to be burnt, though that'd be hard to see in this light."

"Will he be *in compost mentis?*" asked Ainsworth. Cobb choked back an involuntary laugh, and Ainsworth frowned and went on, "I mean *in compos mentis*. When we get him back to the lab, we need him to answer a lot of fairly complex questions."

Lab, thought Cobb. The empty office next to yours, where you've set up your special project—a makeshift Faraday cage, a bottle of rum, a bag of Hershey Kisses and a car battery.

"It wouldn't be *him*," said Cobb, "it'd be his *ghost*. It wouldn't be likely to have much of a mind, but it ought to have most of his memory."

Ainsworth nodded. "His memory is what we want. What he took away with him." He looked around nervously at the lawn and the dark trees. "Before we catch him he'll be loose—he won't transmigrate into one of our bodies, will he?"

He didn't want *any* body, at the end, thought Cobb. And if he were to take one of us now—a trick he carelessly told you he knew how to do!—it would hardly be yours.

"It won't be him," Cobb said again. "I don't see how it could...have agency, be purposeful."

Blaine reached into his briefcase again, and lifted out a steel thermos bottle. He unscrewed the cap and held onto it while he lifted the bottle to sniff its contents. Then he swirled it and said, "I believe your Hershey Kisses have dissolved in the rum."

"That's okay," said Cobb, "it's still chocolate and ethanol—what draws ghosts, he said." With a reluctance that surprised him, he added, "Be ready to slap the cap back on...when he goes in." If he manifests at all, he thought; if ghosts really do go for that odd diet, and he dives in like a genie into a bottle; if he doesn't just dissolve on the wind.

"He won't be able to evade us this time," whispered Ainsworth. "Where do you hide when *death* wouldn't conceal you?"

Cobb paused, a new and disquieting question forming in his mind, but Blaine gestured with the thermos bottle cap. "Go on, go on!"

"...Right." Cobb dropped the cigarette and ground it out under his heel.

He took a deep breath, then stepped up beside the chain-link gate and lifted the strange slide rule. He briefly thumbed the slide and the cursor, then tilted the object to peer through the lenses and nudge the cursor another half an inch, and a moment later tilted it again to squint at the musical note.

E. The *mi* in *do re mi*.

"*Aahhh…*"

He hadn't realized how self-conscious he would be. A moment after he opened his mouth and began singing the note, the absurdity of the whole situation nearly made him toss the crazy slide rule away and break out laughing; but awareness of the two anxious old men standing nearby sobered him. And the slide rule seemed to vibrate faintly in his hand, as if the tiny lenses really were rotating.

He took seven paces forward, then dutifully paused to work the slide and the cursor again. Over the course of the next full minute he sang notes four times, and walked in an angular course all the way around the gate on the grass; and then he paused and lowered the slide rule.

He exhaled, then said, "All the lenses are black."

The three men stared down at the chain-link gate on the grass. Blaine was shakily holding the thermos bottle out in front of himself in his right hand, while in his left he held the cap poised to slap down over the open top of it, and Cobb could hear Ainsworth's quick, wheezing respiration. Peripherally he noticed that the clockwise course the slide rule had led him on formed a five-sided polygon.

Cobb's face was hot, and he wished very much that he had not come along on this expedition, "service to the university" or no.

The wind had started up again sometime during Cobb's ritual pacing, and so it was hard to tell if the branches of the distant trees were really moving, or rippling with distortion in the air, and Cobb clenched his teeth in a sudden colder gust—a rapid snapping started up nearby, like sparks jumping across a gap, and stopped after a few seconds—the zig-zag lengths of chain-link wire began rattling—

And then all three men jumped back, for a woman in jeans and a white blouse had fallen a short distance onto the chain-link gate and collapsed, rolling over onto the grass face down. Her sneakers had dented the center of the chain-link rectangle, silencing it.

For several seconds no one spoke. The woman lay motionless. Then Ainsworth slapped Cobb across the face. "That's not him!" the old man choked.

Cobb had dropped the slide rule. "I *know* it's—" he began, but Ainsworth had spun away to face Blaine.

"How am I ever to get a renewing transfer?" Ainsworth demanded shrilly. "And you're near the end of your line too." He turned again toward Cobb, who was now crouching over the woman.

The old man waved his fists in the air, and went on, "Is it a dead woman? Is this a *joke* of his?"

"Shut up a minute," said Cobb shortly.

He had rolled the woman onto her back, and the buttons on her blouse visibly lifted and sank, lifted and sank—she was breathing, though her eyes were closed and she had rolled over slackly. He brushed long dark hair away from her narrow face and touched her throat over the carotid artery, and he felt a strong unhurried pulse. She looked to be about thirty years old.

"She's unconscious," he said.

"That's—" began Blaine; "I know her! That's his daughter!"

Ainsworth had sat down in the grass, breathing noisily. "Are you sure? How could—"

"Of course I'm sure! I followed her and photographed her two months ago, when we were trying to get him to work with us."

Ainsworth swiveled his head from side to side, and whispered, "Has he shown up too?"

All three of the men glanced around quickly. After a few moments, "No sign," said Blaine. He looked down at the thermos bottle in his hand, then hastily screwed the cap back onto it and dropped it into the briefcase.

"Let's get out of here," said Ainsworth, beginning to struggle to his feet. "This was a failure."

Cobb straightened up, breathing hard and trying to think past the comprehension that they actually had accomplished *some* kind of transmigration here. "We—should call 911." He nodded; that much was clear. "She may be injured, we don't know what happened to her." He reached toward the phone in the hip pocket of his jeans.

Ainsworth was standing, though still bent sharply at the waist. "Leave her here! And the gate too!"

Cobb had his phone in his hand, but Blaine reached across and gripped his wrist. "She *looks* fine," he said. "Maybe we could—"

"Tuck twenty dollars in her pocket," said Ainsworth, straightening up in stages and starting toward the van, "and she can call a cab when she wakes up."

Blaine rocked his head judiciously.

Cobb stared at the two of them. After a few seconds he said, "Well for one thing, there were security cameras at the Newport Boulevard gate. They certainly got the license number of the van. And you," he said, turning to Blaine, "signed out for it. Whatever state she's in, they'd connect her with our visit here."

Cobb could see a gleam of sweat on Blaine's forehead. "You felt her pulse?" the old professor asked.

"Yes, it's normal. But—"

"We'll take her home. I know where she lives. We can't risk the kind of attention—"

"She should go to a hospital! God knows what—"

"Peter and I will take her home," Blaine said firmly. "I'm sure she's only fainted. Very natural, probably. You can stay here and call 911 if you like, after we've taken her away. And whatever you say about this evening's activity, of course, Peter and I will categorically deny." He smiled and touched Cobb's arm. "Who will they believe? Think, son."

Cobb took a moment to imagine what he would say to police. *There was an unconscious woman here, but two professors from Cal State knew who she was, and they're driving her home now; no, I don't know her name, or where she lives, and they'll deny the whole thing anyway.* Or, *We conjured her out of thin air, while we were trying to raise her father's ghost.*

"Okay," he said, exhaling, "okay—we take her home. You'll need my help lifting her into the van anyway." He pocketed his phone, then held up one hand. "But if her pulse or breathing go funny, or she has a seizure or something, we call 911 and detour straight to a hospital."

"Of course," Blaine assured him, slapping him on the back now. "Smart lad."

Ainsworth stamped his foot, nearly losing his balance. "But what if she should wake up on the way?" He blinked down at the unconscious woman. "We could drive her right now to somewhere that hasn't got cameras. Leave her there while she's still unconscious." He looked up. "We *could* even give her a conk right now—just to make sure?"

Blaine glanced at Cobb, then quickly looked away. He shook his head. "This has meant a lot to both of us, Peter," he said quietly, "and it's understandable to get excited and anxious. But—no. Collect yourself." He gave Ainsworth an intense look, then shrugged. "If she wakes up, we'll tell her we found her unconscious at...in her father's office, at the university. Let *her* worry about how she got *there*."

Ainsworth was still frowning, but he gave a jerky, reluctant nod, and then waved impatiently at Cobb and the woman at their feet.

Cobb looked away from the two men, unhappily aware that he could not work with either of them again...and that they would probably insist on the same, after this evening's fiasco. Two years on the tenure track derailed, wasted.

"Dr. Blaine," he said wearily, "you and I can lift her back onto the chain-link, and then we can drag it like a travois back to the van." He glanced toward the boulevard, and added, "*Uh* oh."

The close-set headlights of the security guard's electric cart were weaving up the central lane in their direction.

"I guess we say we found her here," said Cobb, relieved. "True, really." He took a couple of steps across the grass and bent down to retrieve the slide rule and tuck it into his back pocket by his phone.

"No," said Blaine quickly, clutching his briefcase to his chest, "you think of some other story, or Peter and I—we'll say we found the *two* of you here—we'll say you didn't come in the van with us, the guard didn't see you back there—we interrupted you attacking her—"

Ainsworth looked back, silhouetted now against the approaching headlights. "That's right," he croaked. "Rapist."

Cobb coughed out one syllable of an incredulous laugh. "That's—are you kidding?—you can't—"

"Trust me," said Blaine, "we will. Registered sex offender forever." The old man was panting. "Unless you think of a way to keep her identity out of it. Think!"

Cobb crouched, and slid his arms under the woman's knees and ribs; and panic gave him the strength to straighten his legs and stand up, carrying the limp body. Her head hung slack, showing him only her throat and uptilted chin.

He had taken three labored, clumping steps across the grass toward the open back of the van when the electric cart rolled into view on the other side of it.

Cobb couldn't see the driver past the headlights, but kept walking stolidly toward the van, and when his shins collided with the bumper, he carefully leaned forward and laid the woman on her side in the bed of the van.

"What happened?" came the voice of the security guard behind him. "Who's she?"

Cobb turned around; the security guard had got out of his cart and was hurrying toward the van.

"My wife is part of our team," replied Cobb in as calm a voice as he could muster. "She inhaled some of the tantric carbonate—it's not dangerous, but we're taking her down the hill to Chapman Global Medical... just to be sure."

"I'll call an ambulance," said the guard, reaching for the radio on his belt, but Cobb forced a smile and shook his head.

"We've called ahead, they're waiting for us at the hospital. We'll have her there in the time it'd take an ambulance to get here. And we've got emergency inhalers in the van."

"O-kay," said the guard, visibly relaxing. "She's—all right, is she?"

"No danger," rasped Ainsworth.

"It happens," Cobb said. "She'll probably be awake and alert again before we even get there." He turned back to the van and pushed the woman's legs forward out of the way, then climbed up to crouch beside her. "We'd better get moving," he told his two companions.

"Still," said the security guard, reaching again for his radio, "I'd better—" Then he glanced to the side and said, "What's that?"

Cobb saw that the man was pointing at the chain-link gate lying on the moonlit grass.

"We were going to ask you that," Cobb said. "It seems to be part of a fence."

"Azoles must have dragged it in," ventured Blaine, blinking rapidly.

"Well *I'm* not moving it." The guard was scowling. "I'm not paid to clean the place up."

Blaine stepped forward and closed the van's back door; Cobb heard him say, "Quite right. And now we really must..."

A few moments later Blaine and Ainsworth had got back into the van and closed their doors, and Blaine started the engine.

"Turn on the heater," said Ainsworth.

Blaine shifted the van into gear and let the vehicle roll forward. "Does this lane loop back to the main one?"

"Yes," said Ainsworth. "The heater?"

Blaine reached over to push the heater lever all the way to the right.

"Tantric carbonate!" said Ainsworth derisively.

"It was good enough to satisfy the guard," said Blaine. "You and I couldn't think of anything at all."

"You were," said Cobb, trying to keep his voice level, "going to accuse me of attempted rape."

"No no, my boy!" exclaimed Blaine, peering ahead through the windshield. "Never—really! I do apologize for pretending to threaten you. Good heavens, if we'd actually accused you of that, her identity would have been discovered, and that's what we needed to prevent."

"It's like pulling a gun on someone," Cobb persisted. "It doesn't matter if it's loaded or not—you still pulled a gun on him. On me."

"Get over it," advised Ainsworth. "You're committed now anyway—you lied about her to the guard."

"I really do apologize," said Blaine. "Your, yes, *commitment* has been essential tonight, even though things...didn't go as we'd hoped."

"Went all wrong, to be precise," said Ainsworth. "Slide rule!"

Cobb had already concluded that his career at the university was finished, and now he wondered how he could possibly even get through the rest of the night without having to call the police.

"Why would that be so...catastrophic?" he asked dully. "If her identity was found out?"

"Oh," said Blaine, "we're in tentative correspondence with a number of allied institutions; and when we begin to apply his, that is, our, research to practical ends, money will be required, quite a good deal of it, probably, and—"

"A proper lab," put in Ainsworth, "computers, power, housing for subjects..."

"For animal testing!" Blaine interjected hastily. "And we've applied for grants—

National Institute of Health, National Science Foundation—"

"Women and Minorities in STEM Fields," rasped Ainsworth, "The Human BioMolecular Atlas Program..."

"—and any irregularities in our behavior, even eccentricities—"

"Like trying to raise ghosts," put in Ainsworth. "Even uselessly!"

"—would certainly prove detrimental."

Blaine started to say something more, hesitated, and then said, thoughtfully, "We did accomplish *something*, here, you know."

He didn't speak again until the guard had steered his electric cart back to the dark information center and quickly opened the gate for them, and the van had moved forward down the driveway and the turn signals were indicating a left turn onto Newport Boulevard.

"I think it worked," Blaine said finally as he swung the van out onto the lanes and accelerated. "I think that's *him*. Transmigration of souls, right? That was what he was working on, what he wouldn't tell us about—that's why we came here to get him. I think we *did!* I think he transmigrated into the body of his daughter."

Ainsworth grunted in surprise. "You think so?"

"This," said Blaine, freeing a hand from the steering wheel to gesture behind him, "*is* who answered the summons. I believe the slide rule functioned correctly after all."

"Then he really does know how to do it," breathed Ainsworth. "He did it himself. Suicide, sure, why not—who needs the relinquished body?"

Blaine sighed. "Can't take him back to the lab in the thermos bottle now."

"No, but..." Cobb saw the dark blot that was Ainsworth's head shift, clearly turning to look into the back of the van, and in the momentary sweep of a streetlight the expression on his lean old face was avid—hungry. "Easier to question him when he's in a body," he murmured. "It's got nerves."

Blaine glanced at Cobb in the rear-view mirror. "This is all hypothetical, of course," he said. "Considering all conceivable possibilities."

Ainsworth turned away, looking forward again. "Right," he said hollowly. "Not *proposing* anything."

Cobb looked down at the unconscious woman's face, dimly visible when the van passed under a street light, and he wondered if it could really be Armand Vitrielli's soul behind it. *Something* impossible had happened tonight.

And as the van rocked down the boulevard toward the lights of downtown Orange, he considered some of the things these demented old men had said tonight: *I followed her and photographed her two months ago, when we were trying to get him to work with us—He won't be able to evade us this time—where do you hide when* death *wouldn't conceal you?*—

The interior of the van was warming up, but Cobb shivered and felt sick.

Had Blaine and Ainsworth used Vitrielli's daughter as some sort of leverage, to coerce the old man into telling them things he would not otherwise reveal to them? Transmigration of souls...Ainsworth had said, *How am I ever to get a renewing transfer?*

Had Vitrielli chosen to kill himself, rather than either give them what they wanted, on the one hand, or see some intolerable attentions paid to his estranged daughter, on the other?

Or had his concern been solely for the health of her youthful living body, rather than for the daughter who inhabited it?

No; the old man who had been Cobb's friend would not have evicted his daughter's soul from her body, to renew his own life.

If such things were in fact actually possible! But...something conventionally impossible *had* happened tonight.

Cobb looked at the two heads that bobbed against the intermittently lit windshield. Had these two old university professors really driven Vitrielli to suicide—and were they actually now intending to *torture* the body they imagined Vitrielli's soul occupied?

Quietly he reached around and slid his phone out of his back pocket; and the slide rule came free too, and clattered on the corrugated metal of the van's floor.

"Give us your phone," said Ainsworth distinctly. "Now."

"And the slide rule!" added Blaine, extending his right hand back between the front seats. "It's university property, hand it over."

And at that moment the woman groaned, and sat up abruptly and scrambled around onto her hands and knees. "What the hell's going on?" she said.

III

Back in the cemetery, the security guard drowsed in his cart by the gates. For several minutes the only sound around the Vitrielli grave a hundred yards away was the wind in the branches.

A dusting of white frost briefly touched the raised letters and the ceramic portrait on the brass plaque, and the cold air above it rippled, and a brisk snapping briefly broke the quiet; the plaque shivered, and the agitation in the air over the grave coalesced into the outline of a man. The figure's translucent head leaned to one side—and then the thing wavered away across the newly-shriveled grass toward the boulevard.

III

The van slewed from side to side before Blaine got it under control again.

"Cobb!" barked Ainsworth. "Restrain him!"

"I'm doing nothing!" Cobb almost wailed.

"Dr. *Ainsworth?*" said the woman. "Where are we? Is my dad here?" She glanced at Cobb and then scuttled to the right side of the van to see the driver. "Dr. Blaine!"

"You're not deceiving us, Armand!" said Ainsworth. "Restrain him, Cobb, damn you!"

The woman quickly looked around the dim van interior. "My dad's not here," she said. Her voice was taut with evident control. "What's happened? Where is he?"

"Your act is pitiful, Armand!" said Ainsworth. "Your daughter wouldn't have known us! We've never met her!" To Blaine he added, "Don't slow down, he might try to jump out."

The woman turned to Cobb. "Is he talking on Skype or something?"

"He's talking to you," said Cobb miserably. "They both think you're your father. Occupying your body after his suicide."

"*Suicide?* My father? When?"

"Two months ago," Cobb told her. Apparently she had somehow not heard about it. She and her father *were* said to have been estranged. "I'm sorry."

She looked down at herself and patted her blouse and jeans. "What's the date?" she demanded.

"Tuesday," said Cobb, "the 8th of May."

"2018?"

"2018," he confirmed.

She exhaled. "Wh—are you all *insane?* I saw my father an hour ago! He came home from the university and went into his study—as far as I know, he's still there!" She stretched a hand toward Cobb. "Give me your phone."

"Don't do it!" said Ainsworth, but Cobb handed it to her.

Her face was underlit in a frown as she tapped in a number; then it was in shadow again as she held the phone to her ear. After a few seconds Cobb heard the multiple beep and the recorded voice saying that her call could not be completed.

She lowered the phone and stared at the screen, then tossed it back to Cobb and hiked herself forward and gripped the back of the driver's seat. "Dr. Blaine, tell me, please—*what* is going *on* here? How did I *get* here? Did I have a seizure or something?"

In the rear view mirror Cobb could see Blaine's teeth bared in a grimace of indecision. "But how can you know me?" the old professor burst out. "I've never met you!"

She sat back on her heels. "Okay. What is this." Quietly she went on, "You've been over to the house dozens of times." She looked at the other man. "Dr. Ainsworth, you too—both of you were there for dinner on Saturday—you argued with him. I made lasagna."

"Why are you—" began Ainsworth, but didn't finish the sentence.

The woman jerked around to look at Cobb. "And who are you?"

"Clive Cobb, ma'am. An assistant professor. I was doing research for your father."

"Till his *suicide* two months ago, I suppose!"

All Cobb could do was shrug and nod. "You're, uh, his daughter?" he said. "I mean, I gather you are."

"Yes. Meditation Allegra Vitrielli." Speaking more loudly toward the front of the van, she added, "*Not* Armand Antonio Vitrielli, you—pair of—!" She shook her head and turned back to face Cobb. "Please tell me how I ended up in this damned truck or whatever it is."

Cobb hesitated, then said, "We found you unconscious in the cemetery." He nodded back in that direction, aware of Ainsworth shaking his head.

She stared at Cobb. "The cemetery where my father is buried, I suppose."

"Well—yes."

"And where," she asked, "are we going?"

"I believe we're taking you home."

"That's good, at least. What time is it?"

Cobb pushed the stem on his watch and looked at the glowing face. "Just after ten-thirty."

"My dad will be getting worried. But I can bring him out to show you all!" Squinting to see Cobb more clearly in the dim interior of the van, she asked him, "How did I get to the cemetery?"

"I *honestly* don't know."

"Were you—" She apparently gave up on framing a useful question, and just shook her head.

Then for a full minute no one spoke—though at one point and another both the woman and Dr. Blaine opened their mouths and, after a moment, closed them, and Cobb thought he could almost hear the gears spinning furiously in everyone's heads—and the van rattled down Chapman Avenue now, past a freeway overpass and strip malls and a car dealership lit like a carnival. Blaine steered into the left lane to turn south onto Tustin Avenue.

"He wouldn't make up a crazy story like this," said Blaine finally. "It makes no sense at all."

"Maybe," said Ainsworth, waving a hand, "a crazy story...I don't know."

"This isn't the way to the house," said the woman.

"Oh, just *shut up,* for the love of God," said Blaine. "I know where you live!"

"Where's the last place you recall being?" ventured Cobb. "Before you woke up in this van?"

"What? Oh—yes, I was going to see if the mail had come yet."

"I mean where were you? At home?"

"Yes, where the *mailbox* is—and it's north of here, why are we going south?"

"We're going," said Blaine in a strained voice, "to your house on La Veta, where you *do live,* where you have lived for many years, with your daughter. Remember?" He swung the van into a right turn so sharply that Cobb fell against the woman.

"Sorry," he gasped, trying to pull himself away without touching her unnecessarily, "Miss Vitrielli."

She put the palm of her hand against his chest and pushed him back to his previous position. "Everybody calls me Taysha," she told him. "Only nuns ever called me Miss

Vitrielli." To the back of Blaine's seat she said, "And I don't have a daughter, on top of everything else. After this *detour,* will you take me back to the house, on Nohl Ranch Road? Or give me money so I can get a cab to take me there?"

"You tell her, Cobb," said Ainsworth. "You were there to get your, your malfunctioning gate."

"Here we are," said Blaine, slowing and steering into the driveway of a one-story ranch-style suburban house. A new Honda Accord was parked at the right side of a driveway that extended to the left and stretched up past that side of the house. Curtains glowed yellow in a front window, and a porch light shone on a couple of wicker chairs.

Vitrielli's daughter gave Cobb a cautious look as Blaine switched off the engine. "Tell me what?"

Blaine and Ainsworth had opened their doors and were carefully climbing down to the cement driveway.

Cobb heard the two old men outside, clopping toward the back of the van. "Oh hell, Miss—"

"Taysha."

"Taysha. Your father's house was torn down. It's just cleared dirt there now."

"Uh huh." Her voice was flat and impatient. "Within the last hour, since I opened the gate to get the mail. Shit. Give me money for a cab."

Cobb blinked. "Were you *holding* the gate? The last thing you remember, before this?"

"I wish I'd held on tighter. Who do you suppose *does* live here? Give me fifty, to be on the safe side. I'll pay you back."

Blaine or Ainsworth was fumbling at the handle on the outside of the door.

"Did you usually get the mail?" asked Cobb.

"Always, my dad would just let it pile up in the box. Fifty?"

The van's back door was pulled open, and cold, jasmine-scented air swept through the interior. Cobb pocketed the slide rule and then hopped down out of the van and extended his hand toward Taysha.

"I'm fine," she said crossly, and slid down to the pavement without help.

"Do you have your key?" Blaine asked her, clutching his briefcase and glancing up and down the street.

"I don't even have a key to my actual house," Taysha told him, "I wasn't planning to go out."

Blaine hissed through his teeth and hurried up the steps to the front door.

It was pulled open before he could try the knob, and a woman was standing just inside, staring out at them, backlit by the flickering glow of a television. She wore a housecoat over a sweater and a plaid skirt, and her dark hair was pulled back in a pony tail, but she was otherwise identical to Meditation Allegra Vitrielli.

III

Blaine and Ainsworth simply stood there speechless, so Cobb cleared his throat and stepped forward.

"Ms. Vitrielli?" he said.

"Gorba," said the woman in the doorway. "It used to be Vitrielli. What is it?"

Cobb heard Taysha whisper, *"Gorba?"*

He took a deep breath. "We're from Cal State, the university, Ms., ah, Gorba. I'm Clive Cobb, an assistant professor in the Consciousness Research Department, and these gentlemen are colleagues of your—of Armand Vitrielli." He waved toward the two old professors.

The taller of them glanced hesitantly at Cobb, then gave the woman a flickering smile, and bowed. "Dr. Aubrey Blaine, head of the department."

The woman nodded uncertainly. "You were in the paper, in the article about him."

Ainsworth still hadn't managed to straighten up all the way. He hunched forward, nodded, and said, in a scratchy voice, "Dr. Peter Ainsworth, ma'am—Dr. Peter

Ainsworth—we're—we hoped to—we should have called first—"

Taysha edged past Ainsworth into the light. "And I'm Meditation Allegra Vitrielli."

Gorba opened her mouth but didn't say anything. Warm air from behind her carried the smell of—Cobb sniffed—yes, it seemed to be lasagna.

Cobb spread his hands. "Could we come in?"

Gorba was staring at Taysha. "Are you supposed to be my twin or something?"

"That's the only thing that makes sense," said Taysha. Her arms were down at her sides, her fists clenched. "And I do mean the *only* thing. What's your name? Your maiden name."

"What you just said. Meditation Allegra Vitrielli. Uh—people call me Allegra."

"Why would he name us both the same?" Taysha glared at Blaine and Ainsworth, then looked again at Allegra. "I'm called Taysha, generally."

Tim Powers

Allegra slowly raised her hand and bit her knuckle. "My father used to call me that."

"Could we come in?" repeated Cobb.

"He's dead," said Allegra softly. "These two months I've just wanted closure…"

"He's not dead where *I* come from," said Taysha.

Cobb's chest suddenly felt coldly hollow, and his pulse was ringing in his ears. "God help us," he whispered; then more loudly he said, "I think that's the point." He raised his eyebrows at Allegra.

Allegra dropped her hand and looked past them at the empty dark street, clearly wishing it had not yielded up this crazy, unexpected entanglement. At last she sighed and stepped back, opening the door more widely.

Because no one else moved, Cobb stepped up onto the porch, then walked past Allegra into a living room lit by lamps on either side of a gray fabric-covered couch to his left, and, ahead of him, a TV set mounted between drawers and shelves in a big walnut cabinet. An undersized pink

58

bicycle leaned against one corner of the cabinet, and some CNN news show flickered on the TV screen.

The others had followed him in and were standing together on the nondescript tan rug in the middle of the room. Allegra closed the door with evident reluctance, then crossed to the low table in front of the couch and picked up a glass.

"Sit down, I guess," she said. "I'm having a drink, and I think I'll have another after that. Anyone else? Twin?"

"That's Maker's Mark," said Taysha with certainty; and when Allegra nodded, she added, "I'll have the same, thanks."

Blaine had sat down gingerly on the couch, with his briefcase on his lap. "Do you have any brandy?"

"Bourbon," said Allegra. She pursed her lips. "I could make coffee."

"Bourbon will do," Blaine said; and Ainsworth, and then Cobb, nodded. Allegra picked up a remote and turned off the television, then stepped out of the room.

Tim Powers

"You said 'that's the point,'" said Blaine quickly to Cobb. "Tell me what you meant."

Cobb waited, nervously considering the idea that had occurred to him a few moments ago, while Allegra clanked things around in the kitchen; she came back, set a squat bottle and a bowl of ice on the table and returned to the kitchen. This time she reappeared with four glasses. She moved her own drink to a desk in the corner and sat down in the office chair in front of it.

"I turned off the oven," she said. "I'm afraid I can't ask you to stay for dinner. My daughter is due home any time, and I don't want her—"

"You lay the pasta strips down dry, right?" interrupted Taysha. "So they boil right in the lasagna while it bakes."

"That's how he..." Allegra sighed and looked at the ceiling.

Ainsworth lowered himself onto the couch beside Blaine. Cobb and Taysha remained standing.

"Well?" said Blaine to Cobb.

"Okay." Cobb gave Allegra an apologetic, self-conscious glance. "Okay, this will sound crazy, I'm sorry, but—remember the sort of work your father did." He took a deep breath. "The three of us," he said, waving toward the couch, "were in Holy Sepulchre cemetery tonight, trying to summon up the ghost of Armand Vitrielli." He had had to raise his voice in the middle of the sentence, for Ainsworth had begun sputtering and perhaps trying to get up. The two women were just frowning at Cobb as if he'd made an obscene joke. "The procedure," Cobb went on doggedly, "required, among other things, some metal object that Dr. Vitrielli would have handled a lot, and I had fetched the chain-link gate that used to be at the bottom of his driveway."

"He's lying," said Blaine, "or crazy, poor fellow. Obviously. We never—"

"But instead of a ghost," Cobb went on, overriding him, "Taysha appeared, unconscious. From nowhere, out of thin air! These two...*old fools,* to put it kindly, decided that Dr. Vitrielli had taken over her body, and so by catching her they had caught him after all."

"They did think that," said Taysha. "Idiots."

Cobb looked across the room at Allegra. "When's the last time you touched that gate?"

Allegra's mouth had sagged open and her eyes darted from the old men on the couch to Taysha; at last she focused on Cobb. "What? The gate down by the driveway? What on earth are you talking about?" When Cobb didn't answer, she shrugged and said, "Not since I moved out, twelve years ago."

"Taysha, though," resumed Cobb, "handled it every day—was holding it only about half an hour ago—in the real, divergent reality she came from. Universe, say." Everyone began talking, or at least exclaiming, and Cobb held up his hands. "The procedure!—designed by your father," he said to both women, "—was supposed to cleave a gap in our reality, open a trap-door, so to speak, and effect the transmigration of a soul connected to that old chain-link gate, from one world to another. It did." He suppressed a crazy urge to giggle, and turned to Blaine. "I think tonight we inadvertently proved Everett's 'many worlds' interpretation of quantum mechanics. Or at least two worlds. Think about it."

He tried and failed to come up with anything more to say, so he just nodded in conclusion, then crouched beside the table to pour bourbon into one of the glasses. Ice? he wondered. Why bother.

Blaine closed his eyes for a moment, then opened them and put on a sorrowful smile. "Our young would-be colleague might find a better use for his imaginative skills in fiction-writing than in academia. Divergent reality, quantum mechanics! *Ghost* raising!" He looked toward Allegra. "I do apologize for inflicting this insensitive sophomoric vulgarity on you, and at such a time. No, I think the truth is more mundane—and sad."

He now looked earnestly up at Taysha. "Of course you didn't...appear out of thin air in a graveyard tonight! Really, does that story make any sense at all? I'll charitably assume Mr. Cobb is on some variety of medication, if not simply drunk."

"Then what—" began Taysha.

Blaine raised a hand. "We found you unconscious in Dr. Vitrielli's office an hour ago, and mistook you for this woman who lives here. I think it's clear that you are...an unacknowledged daughter of our departed colleague. In your grief at the death of your father, you've constructed this fantasy that he's still alive, and you've taken on yourself the delusion that you are in fact this woman, your half-sister—his *acknowledged* daughter—whom, unfortunately facilitating your fantasy, you do closely resemble." He raised one stern white eyebrow at Cobb. "And it's cruel of you, sir, to carelessly encourage her with your, your whimsical imaginings!"

Allegra seemed to find all this convincing; she was looking with evident interest and sympathy toward Taysha—who had backed away toward the front door.

Her eyes were narrowed and she was breathing deeply. Looking past Cobb at Allegra, she asked hoarsely, "Did he really die two months ago? *Killed* himself?"

"I'm sorry! He did!"

"I'm leaving," said Taysha, "and I can outrun any of you." She turned toward the door, then froze, staring at a bookshelf above the TV set.

"That's my book," she said, and, watching the others warily, crossed to the cabinet and pulled a volume free. Cobb leaned forward to peer at the ragged dust-jacket—the book was *Further Adventures of Lad,* by Albert Payson Terhune.

Taysha blew dust off the top page edges and tossed it toward Allegra, who winced and caught it carefully with both hands.

Taysha said, "If there's a pencil drawing of a collie dog on the back flyleaf of that, signed *Taysha,* then I'm *not* going crazy."

"There is," said Allegra faintly, without opening the book. "I drew it when I was about seven."

"So did I."

Taysha leaned back against the cabinet and ran the fingers of both hands through her hair. "And I once shoplifted Justin Timberlake's album, *FutureSex.* I never told anybody."

"Oh my God," whispered Allegra.

"Hah!" Taysha was panting, as if she'd been holding her breath. "You're the liar," she said to Blaine, "not what's-his-name here, Clive." She paced from the kitchen entry to the door and back again. "When I woke up in your van, we were coming west down the hill on Chapman; Holy Sepulchre Cemetery's up there. The university is north, up the freeway. Why are you—"

"A shortcut—" began Ainsworth.

The curtains over the front window brightened, and Cobb heard a car engine close outside.

"My daughter's home!" said Allegra, standing up. "Everybody, *please*—act normal!" She gave Taysha a wide-eyed look, and added, "I'll send her to her room—you hide in my room!" She pointed down a hall to the right of the kitchen.

Taysha was clearly in agreement that she should not meet Allegra's daughter, and hurried away down the hall. The sound of the car engine changed and then receded away.

Blaine struggled to his feet as footsteps tapped up the driveway and onto the porch, and a girl of about ten pushed open the door and hurried into the living room, then abruptly stopped when she saw the visitors.

She was thin and dark-haired, wearing jeans and a white T-shirt, and Cobb thought she looked very like a young Taysha—or Allegra.

Allegra managed a smile. "These are professors from your grandfather's college, Lucy. Say hello and then leave us to talk grownup business."

"You knew him?" the girl asked, looking from Cobb to the two professors. Ainsworth had not got up.

"Oh, yes," said Blaine.

"I never got to." She half-turned toward her mother, then faced Cobb. "Was he a nice man?"

Cobb cleared his throat. "Yes. I liked him."

She held his gaze for a moment, then said, "Hello," to the room at large. She turned away and disappeared down a hall to the left, and a few seconds later they all heard a door close.

"He *is* a nice man," said Taysha quietly, stepping into the living room from the other side of the kitchen. "I'm glad he's still alive...in my world." She was holding the crucifix of a dangling silver-beaded rosary. "This is mine too."

"I've had it forever," said Allegra, too softly for Cobb to guess whether it was agreement or protest.

"In my world," Taysha went on, "the Virgin Mary doesn't have one hand broken off."

"Lucy knocked it off the bedside table one time," said Allegra. "I've meant to glue the hand back on." She gazed down the left-side hall and said vacantly, as if from long habit, "Kids!"

"Kids," echoed Taysha in a hollow voice, also looking down the hall. She gathered the rosary into her palm. "You went ahead and married *Lou Gorba?*" Without waiting for an answer, she turned to Cobb. "So how do I get back there? Home?"

His face was suddenly cold. "Oh," he said. "I'm—not sure. The chain-link gate got used up, according to how your father said these things work...maybe if I flipped it over, and tried to do the ritual in reverse?" Somehow, he thought. "The security guard might let us back into the cemetery, where the gate is, to try." He was ruefully aware that he sounded hopeless.

"Not in the university van!" objected Blaine. "We can't participate in these hurtful fantasies."

Allegra cast an anxious glance down the hall toward her daughter's room, and said, "Can't you all just *leave?*"

"Do *you* think we can?" asked Taysha.

Allegra met her duplicate's gaze, then sighed. "Let's take this out back. Bring your drinks and the bottle."

Blaine helped Ainsworth up off the couch, and Allegra led the way through the kitchen and pushed open a back door.

Outside, lit by a couple of lamps under the eaves, half-a-dozen plastic-webbing chairs were arranged around a wrought-iron table on a narrow patio, and to the left the old gray Buick that Cobb had worked on so often was parked at the top end of the driveway. Cobb set the bottle and his glass on the table and slumped into one of the chairs.

▌▌▌

Out in front of the house, the driver's side door of the van slowly swung open, and the interior light came on, and then after a few seconds the door closed and the light went out again.

▌▌▌

Taysha pointed at the Buick as she stepped down from the kitchen doorway. She was still holding the rosary.

"That's Dad's car. You've been driving it?"

"Just one time, from the university. It smells like his old pipes."

Blaine and Ainsworth tottered outside right behind her, carrying glasses, and Blaine crossed to the table, picked up the bottle and poured a generous slosh of bourbon into his. Ainsworth fidgeted impatiently beside him.

Taysha sat down in the chair next to Cobb, and the rosary rattled as she laid it on the table. "You've got cigarettes," she said to him. "Bum one?"

Cobb pulled the pack of Camels from his shirt pocket and dug in his jeans for the lighter. She pulled a cigarette from the pack and took the lighter from him, and a moment later she was leaning back in her chair, exhaling a plume of smoke.

She glanced back toward the kitchen. "Is he going to show up?" she asked Allegra. "Lou," she added, when Allegra gave her an alarmed look.

"Oh, him," said Allegra. She had shuffled a few steps out across the patio, but kept glancing back at the house as if she might run back inside. "We're divorced. Three years now. He's in Oregon."

"I can't believe you married him! *I* told him to get lost after he had that big fight with Dad."

"Oh, I nearly did, too," sighed Allegra, "but Dad started it—he provoked him, picking on him about his biker tattoos, remember?"

Cobb was surprised to see that Allegra was apparently accepting his theory, and he wondered how much she had had to drink before they arrived.

Taysha nodded. "He wanted me to get one, too, and Dad wouldn't stand for that." She tapped ash from her cigarette and gave Allegra an inquiring look.

Cobb saw Allegra's face redden. "I have Lucy," she said, quietly but defiantly.

Taysha opened her mouth, then closed it. After a moment she went on, "But you left Dad alone in that house? Did you think he could manage by himself?"

"I have my own life!" protested Allegra. "We had a big fight about Lou. Dad said he was a bum, and I called Dad a has-been loser who couldn't keep his wife. But it was true! And he drank!"

Taysha angrily pointed her cigarette at the drink in Allegra's hand and was clearly about to make an obvious rejoinder, but the creak of a car door opening stopped her.

And then a windy whisper from the left said, *"I did."*

Every head whipped around toward the Buick, and Taysha's cigarette went flying; the passenger door was open now, and a filmy silhouette inside was visible only because it was moving. A glassy distortion at the bottom edge of the door frame implied a lowered leg, and then part of the roof seemed to ripple as the silhouette straightened up.

Allegra sat right down on the cement, her eyes wide and her hands over her mouth; Cobb would have stood up, but Taysha had clamped a hand on his upper arm and was breathing harshly in his ear. He was staring toward the indistinct thing that now stood beside the car; for a moment in his peripheral vision he could see Blaine and Ainsworth, motionless, and then they had retreated out of his sight.

"Hath no man's bottle here a drink for me?" came the ghost's whisper again.

Cobb heard scuffling behind him, and managed to look away from the wavering distortion in the air. Blaine was now trying to open his briefcase, impeded by Ainsworth, who seemed to be trying to help.

At last Blaine fumbled the steel thermos bottle out of his briefcase and was unscrewing the cap. "Here!" he said, "rum and chocolate!"

Ainsworth tried to say something, presumably to coax the ghost, but produced only a spitty wheezing.

Cobb shook his head sharply to clear it. They still want to capture Vitrielli's ghost, he thought, so that they can question it later, learn what Vitrielli chose to die rather than reveal to them. In Ainsworth's words, *How am I ever to get a renewing transfer?*

Taysha let go of Cobb's arm and for a moment closed her eyes; then she opened them and said, fairly steadily, "I'm sure he'd rather have bourbon than whatever that is." She reached for the Maker's Mark bottle.

But the upright patch of distortion had shifted forward, past her, and an expanding spray from its upper limbs might have been ghost fingers extending toward Blaine.

"Sweeter," breathed the ghost.

"See," said Blaine, "he wants this stuff!" He waved the thermos with one shaking hand, holding the cap above it with the other.

He's ready to catch Vitrielli like a moth in a bottle, thought Cobb; and he got up and stepped around the side of the table away from the ghost, waving Blaine back, and all he could think of to say was, "You don't serve him in a glass?"

Allegra had got unsteadily to her feet, and she and Taysha both nodded. "He's," quavered Allegra, "a guest."

"There's no extra glass," snapped Blaine, staring over Cobb's shoulder at the apparition and still waving the steel cylinder. "Armand!" he called.

"He can have mine," said Taysha, whose glass was still empty. "I'm not thirsty."

Blaine rocked back and forth, breathing hard and squinting belligerently at Cobb; then his shoulders sagged and he muttered, "Of course, of course—where are my manners."

He shuffled to the table and reluctantly leaned over it to pour some of the brown liquid into Tasha's glass; but he hovered nearby, and Cobb thought he was positioning himself to slap his hand over the top of the glass.

Taysha may have thought the same, for she lifted the glass and held it away. She looked up at the blur hovering over her and in a husky voice said, "Here you go, Dad."

"Mirrors on the grass, alas," whispered the ghost.

It seemed to shrink, and Cobb realized that it must have been bending over the glass that Taysha was holding out. And the brown liquid in the glass jiggled, and its level might have gone down a fraction of an inch.

And the ghost's form curdled into visibility—Cobb found himself staring at a figure that seemed to be made of white smoke. There were suggestions of a turned-up collar and coat-tails, and its long hair, and fringes on the vague clothing, waved outward as if the figure were under agitated water. Taysha clanked the glass back down onto the table.

"Not mirrors," the ghost said, and its voice, stronger now, was a groan. "Two Tayshas." The oval of the head became a profile, facing one way and then the other. "Blaine and the monkey," the ghost went on. Its form was pulsing, as if it were laboring for breath. "The tape—in the car. Let me go. It hurts."

Ainsworth shook Blaine's arm and gestured toward the ghost, clearly demanding that the other man somehow catch the unnatural thing in the thermos. Certainly more loudly than he meant to, he whispered, "Hurry, it's *speaking!*"

The thing bent and uttered a hoarse cry. Everybody except Taysha flinched, though her eyes glittered with tears.

"What did you kill yourself for?" Her voice was harsh. "Why didn't you come to me?" She touched her chest and then gestured toward Allegra.

The ghost was beginning to fade—Cobb could see the outlines of moonlit trees through its substance. "Enquire of the jokers yonder," it said, more faintly. "Et tu, Clive?"

Cobb flinched. "I'm sorry!" He jerked his head toward Blaine and Ainsworth. *"They* want to catch you when you're drinking the rum and chocolate. Get you into that thermos bottle. Force you to tell them...what you didn't want to tell them before."

"Ah?" said the ghost, retreating from the glass with the brown mix in it. "Still? And which of these Tayshas..." Its voice was hard to hear now.

Taysha quickly grabbed Cobb's glass, and held it up. "Maker's Mark, Dad!"

"My old pal," said the ghost, to the woman or the liquor, and its fading form bent over the raised glass. Cobb couldn't tell whether the liquid in the glass was stirred by the ghost's action or by Taysha's raised and trembling hand, but in seconds Vitrielli's ghost was again an opaque, smoky white silhouette. The glass fell from Taysha's limp fingers and broke on the cement. Cold bourbon splashed on Cobb's ankle.

The ghost's profile was still tilted down toward her, and its rippling hand touched her shoulder, and even managed to twitch back the collar of her blouse. Her eyes were clenched shut, and Cobb saw her knuckles whiten as she gripped the edge of the table.

"No *Ride to Live, Live to Ride?*" croaked the ghost, straightening up. "No panhead rampant?" Cobb recalled that a panhead was an antique Harley Davidson motorcycle.

"I'm," Taysha said through clenched teeth, "the one who didn't marry Lou Gorba."

The ghost moved back from her, and she opened her eyes and hugged herself, gripping her elbows.

"Blaine," said the ghost's voice; and it went on slowly, as if trying to remember

names: "Ainsworth…Cobb. More walls than you knew, broken, eh? To force me here."

Cobb's heart was pounding in his chest, and he was fervently wishing that Vitrielli's reproachful ghost—this wrongly half-awakened thing, this animate evidence of their…betrayal, sacrilege—would just finally disappear. His lips pulled back from his teeth as he recalled conversations he'd had with the man whose ghost this was.

Et tu, Clive?

But a smoky white arm extended toward Allegra. "That one," it said, and Cobb imagined he could see a pained grimace on the featureless oval of its head, "of this house. You would kill her."

"No!" whispered Blaine, and Ainsworth flapped his hands. "No, no, my friend," Blaine went on, more strongly, "we wouldn't have *done* it—it was just a, a *bluff,* to get you to work with us! We need—you need!—youth, health—"

"He killed himself," said Cobb harshly, "to evade your ultimatum. Your blackmail."

Allegra's chin was pulled back, making folds in her neck. "You did it," she whispered to the ghost, "to save me? *Me?*"

Blaine's mouth hung open, and he was still absently waving the thermos. "We never," he was muttering, "never would—"

"I heard a glass break," said a young girl's voice from the kitchen doorway.

Cobb looked up—Allegra's daughter Lucy was stepping down to the patio.

III

"Sweetie, get back in the house!" cried Allegra, spreading her arms as she hurried toward the girl—but Lucy was staring past her, and her eyes were wide.

"That's a ghost," she said distinctly.

"No," babbled Allegra, "it's a, at the college, a hologram, like at Disneyland—"

Cobb saw with relief that the Vitrielli apparition was fading again. When it spoke, its voice was hitching, as if it were in pain:

"What I am," it said, "should not be here."

Go, thought Cobb. Just *go,* poor restless dead, before they do catch you.

Lucy had been staring at the ghost, but now glanced at Taysha, then looked at her more closely; and she turned to her mother. "Are you twins?" she asked quietly; but her mother seemed not to have heard.

Allegra must have noticed the ghost's dimming, for she hurried around the table and held up her glass. "Bourbon," she whispered; "drink, Dad, please! Don't leave me—us!"

The oval of its head, nearly transparent now, hesitated, then quickly dipped toward the liquor. Its silhouette filled out over the course of several seconds, like ice crystals growing in a chilled container of water, but the resulting figure was a foot or so shorter than it had been, and faintly marbled with gray streaks. Cobb thought he heard it groaning faintly.

"I don't belong here either," Taysha said. "In my world I stayed with Dad." But she was looking at Lucy as she spoke, and her voice wavered.

Allegra lowered the glass with which she had renewed the ghost. "I did what I had to do," she said, blinking against tears. "I can't go back."

"I can," said Taysha, with an intense stare at Cobb. "Right?" She picked up his pack of cigarettes and lit another one.

Lucy was simply staring, wide-eyed, at everyone.

"The tape," came the ghost's voice then, tight with evident effort, "for you to find."

"*What* tape?" Cobb burst out.

"The monkey called, said tell him how, or—" The thing seemed to cough, and what had been gray streaks were now gaps in its substance; it partially collapsed, and was now only about three feet tall. Cobb heard Taysha groan softly in sympathy, and realized that he had done the same.

Blaine turned to Ainsworth. "You did it over the *phone?* So he could *record* it?"

Ainsworth backed away from him and bumped the table. "I was circumspect!" he said shrilly, and he snatched up a glass and took a gulp; but it was Taysha's glass, and he choked and spat rum and chocolate down his shirt. "Circumspect!" he whispered, and bent over, gagging.

Blaine quickly shuffled forward and reached out to scoop the suffering, truncated ghost into the thermos bottle, and both women called, simultaneously, *"Look out, Dad!"*

Allegra jerked as if with an electric shock, then steadied herself and stepped in front of Blaine and pushed him back.

"You killed him," she whispered in the old man's face, but a moment later she was blinking around in evident confusion.

"Ach," said Taysha, shoving her chair back and throwing her cigarette away across the grass. "I don't smoke!" She seemed startled to see the rosary in front of her on the table, and picked it up.

Blaine desperately called to the ghost over Allegra's shoulder. "In the car? Where in the car? Under the seat, in the trunk?"

Ainsworth had straightened up. His chin was wet and he was still wheezing, but he lurched around the table toward the ghost. His hands were clawed in front of him, apparently intending to simply tear the suffering apparition to shreds.

"Allegra!" called Allegra. "Stop him!"

Still gripping the rosary, Taysha leaped up from her place at the table and drove a shoulder into Ainsworth's sopping shirt over his chest; with a squeal he went flailing backward.

Then she spun toward where Allegra stood. "I'm—"

"—in the—" said Allegra through clenched teeth.

"—wrong body!" wailed Taysha, pressing her fists to her temples. "Put me back!"

Allegra stepped up in front of Cobb, and her eyes showed white all around the irises.

"What," she said, her voice resolutely level, "the hell—is *this?*"

Cobb looked into her eyes. The woman confronting him wore Allegra's skirt and sweater and housecoat, but he said, with unhappy certainty, "Taysha."

"Yes!" She lifted a hand and dragged her palm across her face and down her throat, and her mouth worked as if she were feeling her teeth with her tongue. She looked past him, evidently meeting the eyes of her own body. "But *that's me,* standing behind you."

Her face blank, Lucy crossed to the woman in jeans and squinted up at her face.

"He did it!" cawed Ainsworth. He turned to the wavering ghost, rubbing his wet chest and grimacing. "Armand, do it for me now, while you can!" He thrust one bony old finger toward Cobb. "Switch me with him! I'll give you more rum!"

Vitrielli's ghost was dimming again. It raised its arms, and with a final diminishing wail it imploded, leaving nothing to be seen. A puff of chilly air swept across the patio.

The rosary dangling from Taysha's fist vibrated into a blur beside her head.

And a rapid clicking started up in the backyard, seeming to come from all directions at once, and the woman in jeans and a white blouse who had been standing beside the table was gone. Lucy stumbled forward a step, reaching toward nothing.

The unsupported rosary flickered through the lamplight and rattled on the cement.

No one moved. For a few seconds the wind in the dark trees at the back of the yard was the only sound.

Lucy backed up till she bumped a chair, and she sat down, shaking her head rapidly. Taysha, in Allegra's body, simply shut her eyes as if replaying the past few moments in protesting memory.

Blaine said, bitterly, "They've both gone back. The interval is closed."

Cobb's face was cold with a sudden dew of sweat as he quickly and uselessly looked around at the house and the patio and the yard. The right body went back to the divergent universe, he thought in horror, but with the wrong woman in it. What—

What have I done?

Ainsworth was panting, possibly with relief. "Get the tape, hurry!" he called to Blaine, swaying and rubbing his chest.

Lucy's hand remained raised, and she was still staring at the empty space where Taysha's body had stood, but she inhaled and said, clearly, "My mom cleaned out that car. Vacuumed under the seats and spare tire and everything. There were some tapes—cassettes—they got thrown out."

Blaine had started toward the Buick, but slid to a halt and looked back at her. "Are you sure? All of them?"

Lucy's lips were pressed together and her gaze was fixed; but after a few seconds she turned to the old professor and said, "I threw 'em out. Nobody listens to cassettes anymore."

"That makes sense," said Blaine eagerly, nodding. To Ainsworth he snapped, "We've got to get out of here, now. This whole evening has been a rout."

It was clear that Ainsworth would need assistance to get back to the van—he was pale, and gulping air—and Blaine glanced toward Cobb and beckoned impatiently.

"I'm not going," said Cobb.

"If you want to save any portion of your career—" began Blaine.

"I don't. Go."

"You may be sure we'll deny—"

"I know. Go."

Blaine rocked his head back and inhaled. "I must demand that you give me my colleague's slide rule. It's university property, and I'll see that charges are brought if you refuse."

Cobb just stared at him.

After several seconds, Blaine lowered his head and frowned at Cobb from under his gray eyebrows, and then he just turned away and got his right shoulder under Ainsworth's left arm. Ainsworth gasped in evident pain, but the two of them went shambling unsteadily away down the driveway.

When the sound of their halting progress finally ended with the closing of two doors and the roar of the van's engine, Lucy looked up at Cobb with narrowed eyes. "Now you make everything back the way it was, you hear?" she said fiercely.

Cobb looked away from her, down at the pavement under his shoes. He was trembling, and his face was cold with sweat, and he couldn't look at her or the woman standing on the other side of the table. Because of my actions, this little girl's mother has been sent God knows where, he thought, and this woman has been pulled out of her world and put in the wrong body—and incidentally the animate revenant of a man I liked and admired has been cruelly tormented—and I can't think of a way to make any of it...back the way it was.

Taysha broke in on his spiraling thoughts. "What slide rule?" Already she looked ill-at-ease in Allegra's skirt and housecoat.

"It's," Cobb began; he took a deep breath and met her intent gaze. "It's how we brought you across. I can work it again, but we had metal that you had touched, that gate—but the gate is used up, and it wouldn't summon *her*, anyway."

"Why did she *disappear?*"

"The interval was over, and she was holding that rosary—it was metal, and it was something she had handled a lot in at least one of the two worlds—aura signature—and she was touching it in this one; so it worked like a trap-door."

He kicked at a piece of broken glass, then made himself face Lucy. "Or a bridge, say," he added hastily. "Did—does—your mother have anything else, metal, that she'd have had before she...got together with your father?"

The girl bit her trembling lip, then glanced back toward the house. "Some books, maybe some clothes," she said. "Metal? I don't know. my father made her get rid of a lot of stuff."

Taysha shivered and pulled Allegra's housecoat more closely about her. "I had a garden," she said, "when I was a little girl—long before Gorba ever showed up— way at the back of the yard, by the fence. I stopped tending it when I was twelve or so. Do you think the old faucet is still out there? Nobody else ever went out to that end of the yard." She snapped her fingers in front of Cobb's face. "The faucet was metal."

"When you were twelve." Cobb blinked at her. He could feel the angularity of the slide rule in his back pocket. "Your lifelines hadn't split yet...in that place and time you were still the one girl." He wiped his face with both hands, then dragged his fingers through his damp hair. "There are still trees at the back end of your father's empty lot, maybe the faucet is still there too." He tried to remember some of old Vitrielli's speculations. "And there's been a lot of strain on the fabric tonight—violations of the Law of Conservation of Reality—if we do it with you holding the faucet, thus aimed *back* to where you *came* from, where you belong, all these violations might very well cancel out, and the realities fall back to their ground states." He gave her what must have been a wild-eyed look; when she took a step back, he hastily smoothed his disordered hair and just nodded, with more confidence than he felt.

"Things," he said distinctly, "would be back the way they were, in other words."

"You're not just...losing your mind, right?"

"No, no."

"Okay." Taysha slapped the pockets of the housecoat. "Keys," she said. She turned to Lucy. "Where did your mom—where does your mom keep her car keys?"

"You can't take her car!" said the little girl, finally beginning to cry. "You're not even her!"

"We're trying to—" Taysha began, then just shook her head and sprinted to the Buick. The door was still open, and she bent to peer inside. "There's a key in this one," she called.

"I'll drive," said Cobb, jumpy and breathless now with the prospect of something, anything, to be done. "It tends to stall when it's cold, unless she got the EGR valve fixed."

Taysha nodded and slid into the passenger seat.

Lucy ran to the kitchen door and closed it, then hurried to the car and pulled open the back passenger-side door. "I'm going," she said as she climbed in and closed the door.

Taysha, in the girl's mother's body, half turned around, her mouth open, but hesitated.

"We can't leave her here by herself," said Cobb, twisting the familiar key in the ignition. The engine chugged, turned over several times reluctantly, then roared. Cobb released the parking brake and clicked the gear shift into reverse.

"Go back up Tustin," said Taysha as she pulled her door shut.

"I know where it is. I spent a lot of evenings there, talking with him." He hooked his arm over her seat and steered backward down the driveway into the dark street. "Drinking Maker's Mark bourbon, in fact." He shifted to drive and sped toward the intersection.

Lucy was sniffling in the back seat. "Did my mother turn off the oven?" she asked.

"Yes," said Cobb, catching a green light and making a squealing left turn north on Tustin Avenue. In the rear-view mirror he saw Lucy sit back, tears still gleaming on her face, frowning and staring out the window at the passing stores and restaurants. He looked away before she might meet his eye.

After a few moments he heard the girl say, "My mom never touched this car after she drove it home. If there was a tape in it, it's still here."

Taysha laughed softly. "Clever girl!"

"You'll want to tell the police about it," said Cobb; "that is, have your mother tell them."

"You tell her, when you get her back."

"Right." He spared a glance at Taysha beside him. "Who's president? Where you come from?"

"Donald Trump," she answered distractedly. Then she turned to him and asked, "How about here? Slow down, will you?"

"The same. Trump." The engine seemed to be running smoothly, and Cobb lifted his foot from the accelerator. "What won the Best Picture Oscar this year?"

"I don't know. *La La Land?* That was big."

"That was last year, and *Moonlight* won. Emma Stone did get Best Actress."

"Oh." She shrugged. "I don't pay a lot of attention to the Oscars."

Despite the weight of his guilty anxiety, Cobb was impatient to find out how her alternate reality might differ from this one. "Who won the World Series?" he asked.

"Beats me. You're going to turn right on Lincoln, but don't get on the freeway."

"I know."

"So who did win the World Series?"

"Never mind. How about—"

From the back seat, Lucy spoke up. "She thought he didn't love her. My grandfather."

"He," said Taysha, tugging Allegra's housecoat around herself, "did what he did, to save her. Me. Us."

"I never even got to meet him," said Lucy. In the rear-view mirror, Cobb saw that she was scowling. "I'll find that tape."

Cobb turned right on Lincoln and sped past the freeway connector lanes to rows of dark houses set back from the street.

"It'll be on your left," said Taysha, pointing with Allegra's hand. Lucy was now leaning forward between the seats.

"Not anymore," said Cobb.

"There it," Taysha began, then fell silent when the flat, empty lot swung into view. A nearby streetlight cast a fan of light that extended past where Cobb recalled the front porch of the house had stood.

"An hour ago—!" breathed Taysha.

"Did his house disappear too?" asked Lucy timidly.

Taysha could only nod.

Cobb steered the Buick onto the rutted patch that had been the bottom of the driveway, and soon he was driving slowly across flat dirt; and he was and thinking about the absent rooms whose spaces he was traversing. Here had stood the kitchen; here the dining room; and here the study, where on so many evenings he had sat across the broad table from Armand Vitrielli, as smoke from the old man's pipe and his own cigarette settled in a faint layer over their heads, and lamplight gleamed on surrounding book spines and two frequently refilled glasses.

Et tu...

He blinked and glanced to the side at Taysha, and guessed that she too was seeing vanished rooms; and he wondered how they differed from the ones he remembered.

After a minute he was sure he had driven past where the back porch had stood—with, in his memories at least, a threadbare old couch and a spare refrigerator and bins of old forgotten clothing—and in the headlight beams he saw the tall laurel trees still standing along the fence at the far end of the lot.

"All the way back," said Taysha hoarsely.

The car had rolled past the wide area of planed-flat dirt now, and was rocking across low ridges and dips. Tall weeds rustled and bent against the bumper.

Taysha was shaking her head. "He always ignores the letters from the county," she said. "It's me that chops the weeds down after every rain."

Tangles of old fallen branches ahead of them shone stark white in the headlight glare. The car slid to a halt, though the engine was still in gear; Cobb gunned it a couple of times, and heard a rear tire spinning in sandy dirt.

He switched off the engine but left the headlights on. "We walk from here," he said. "I can wedge branches under the tires afterward. Lucy, you stay in the car."

"I don't think I'll need headlights," said Taysha.

"I will," he said. .

"Can't I come with you?" pleaded Lucy. "What if his ghost comes back, and wants to sit in here?" The idea had apparently occurred to her even as she had spoken, for her voice had risen sharply by the end of the question.

"Damn it—" Cobb opened his door, flooding the car with cold air that smelled of decaying leaves, "—stand by the car, anyway! We don't want *you* falling into any...*cosmic vortices.*"

Taysha climbed out, gave the girl a semblance of a reassuring smile, and began walking through the weeds toward the back fence. Cobb followed her.

"Careful," she said. "Drag your feet—there's probably still old tomato cages out here." She paused and turned her head from side to side. "I think some of these things are millionth generation onions."

"Find the damn faucet."

"Oh, it's right here." She tapped an upright pipe with Allegra's shoe. "You should have seen this corner of the yard back in 2000 or so. Pumpkins, strawberries..." She looked up at him, her hair backlit by the headlights and her face lost in shadow. "What do we do?"

Cobb sighed. "It'll seem funny," he said, pulling the slide rule from his pocket.

"Funny?"

Abruptly he had no confidence that anything at all would be accomplished here. After half an hour or so of useless stamping around under these trees, he thought, what will we do? Where do we take Lucy? And what will become of Taysha, in Lucy's mother's body? What on *earth* can we possibly *do?*

He forlornly wished they'd brought the bourbon along.

"Go on," said Taysha. "Should I be touching the faucet?"

"Oh—yes. Yes, you might as well hold onto the faucet."

She turned on him, probably glaring. "You *are* gonna *try* here, right?"

Her words shamed him. Yes, he thought, try. "It worked before. Sort of."

He pulled the slide rule from his pocket and held it up. He had to tilt it toward the car's headlights to see which lenses were clear. The car, and Lucy standing beside it, looked very far away though the tiny glass disks.

"Well go on then, grab the faucet," he told Taysha.

He slowly pushed the center bar and shifted his feet around until he could see faint light through all three of the cursor's lenses; it required him to face away from the car, and he had to move his head aside to see the musical note stamped in the wood below it in the headlights' illumination.

D. The *re* in *do re mi*.

Belatedly he realized that he should have told Taysha that he would be vocalizing musical notes; she jumped when he began singing the note, and he freed one hand from the device long enough to wave away any interruption.

He was sweating again as he blinked and squinted and dragged his feet through dry leaves, stepping over fallen branches when he bumped into them, and sang a series of low notes. *A specific sequence of compression frequencies projected in the air, in space and time, in certain directions,* he told himself. *The drawing object will resonate.*

The slide rule in his hand did seem to vibrate, as if the little lenses in it were rotating.

He plodded on, regularly tilting the slide rule to see the indicated notes by the car's lights. It must be nearly midnight, he thought as he sang another note. What can that little girl, Lucy, be thinking of all this?

At one turn he was able to glance to the side, toward the car, and he saw that she was still standing beside the front bumper.

When he had paced—counterclockwise, this time—all the way around Taysha and the faucet, there was no light at all to be seen through any of the lenses, and the tree branches overhead rustled in a sudden cold wind. He was panting, and he could see the steam of his breath.

"Ah!" exclaimed Taysha sharply; she started to fall, and reached out and grabbed Cobb's hand to keep her balance. The slide rule tumbled out of his hand.

But the blackness in the lenses had filled his vision, and engulfed him. His instant of panic gave way to unconsciousness.

III

He became aware that he was lying face-down on twigs and dirt in darkness, and a chilly wind was twitching at his damp hair.

He heard leaves crackle very nearby, and heavy breathing; he rolled to the side in alarm, and by dim moonlight filtering through branches overhead he was able to see that a woman was sprawled in the dirt a yard or so away from him.

Then his memories began falling back into place, like scattered pages restored to order.

"Taysha?" he said hoarsely.

"Yes," she answered, sitting up. "What happened? Did we switch back, is this your, your *ground state?*"

Cobb blinked around at the wide yard, and he could see no one at all—just a patchy lawn and trees and the yellow-lit windows of the house a hundred feet away.

"I don't think—" he began, but Taysha interrupted him.

"There's my house! And the car is gone!"

"Oh," he said. A shrill keening seemed to have started up in his head, and he had to remind himself to breathe. "Yeah."

She exhaled in a long, low whistle. "I'm back, thank God! Look, no weeds! I cut 'em back with a weed-whacker just a week ago, here! *Here!*" She started to get up, then froze, staring at one bare knee; and she clutched at the hem of the plaid skirt she was wearing. "Ach, but I'm still in her body!

She went back, in mine! O God God God."
For several seconds she just crouched, blinking at her knee; then her wide eyes reflected points of amber from the distant windows as she turned to Cobb. "And what are *you* doing here?"

"I guess I," he paused to take a deep breath, "fell through the reality hole with you."

"Terrific."

"Before we—" he began, but Taysha had already stood up and was striding toward the house.

"I'm gonna talk to my dad," she called back.

"Wait, dammit," he said, struggling to his feet, "keep your voice down, we should make sure—"

He hurried after her; and when they had covered half the distance to the house, a figure detached itself from the shadows below the eaves and stepped forward into the oblique light from the windows, waving at them.

Taysha paused, and Cobb caught up with her, panting.

"It's me," she whispered to him. "My body, I mean. She didn't go back after all."

The woman ahead of them, who was indeed wearing Taysha's rightful jeans and white blouse, pointed toward the west corner of the house, and Taysha and Cobb hurried forward and joined her in the shadows there by the driveway. The dusty black Buick Regal that Cobb had worked on so often in the other world stood in front of them; at Cobb's elbow was an open window, and the kitchen within was dark. Faintly, somewhere in the house, he could hear violin music.

"Where is Lucy?" asked Allegra in a tense whisper. She was bracing herself with one hand against the wall, and Cobb saw that she was somehow holding the rosary again.

"She's waiting for us by the car," said Taysha, "Dad's Buick, back in the other... world. Is Dad in the house? Why are you hiding out here?"

"Don't talk so loud!" said Allegra, "Yes, he's in there, *alive,* in his study. I woke up on our bed, in our room! The same old bed! I could hear him, whistling along to Tchaikovsky, the way he always did, and I tip-toed out through the kitchen."

"Where did you get the rosary?" asked Cobb.

Allegra blinked at the silver beads on the string loop. "It was under the pillow."

Taysha nodded impatiently. "That's where I keep it, that's why she wound up in my room, right? Come on, we're going in to talk to him."

"No!" said Allegra, in a whisper that managed to be shrill. "I can't face him! I called him a, a has-been loser who couldn't keep his wife. How can I—"

"That wasn't him," said Taysha. "Not *this* him."

"But it did hurt him. It hurt me." She stared imploringly at the other two. "I'm afraid to! I went to his funeral! I saw his horrible old ghost! Can't you see? He's—"

Tim Powers

And then both women protested, simultaneously, "He's my *dad!*"

Allegra's fist clenched spasmodically on the rosary; Taysha jerked and then swayed against Cobb, who braced an arm around her shoulders to steady her.

The hand holding the rosary opened. "How—"

"—did you get hold of—" gasped the other woman.

"—this?"

The woman in the housecoat stepped hastily away from Cobb, blinking at him with evident mistrust.

And the woman in jeans and a white blouse straightened away from the wall and slapped at her ribs and thighs. She had dropped the rosary. "I'm in—" she began.

"—my own body—" exclaimed Allegra, stepping backward and tugging for reassurance at the lapels of the housecoat.

"—again!" said Taysha, walking hesitantly out across the driveway.

110

Through the open kitchen window came the sound of a door closing somewhere in the house, and the scuff of footsteps on a hardwood floor.

Cobb waved urgently at the two women, and no one spoke until they heard another door close.

"Don't say anything," he whispered. He had just remembered these two women speaking heatedly in unison once before, back on that patio—*Look out, Dad!*—when Blaine had tried to scoop their father's ghost into his thermos bottle. "Your father is where the two of you over-lap—emotionally, psychically. When you both said *Dad* at once, you spilled across, into each other. Both times. We're in an unstable trap-door interval right now—*don't* say it again."

And that first interval ended, he thought, shortly after they had done it on the patio. Allegra, in Taysha's body, had been holding the rosary then—and when the interval ended, she had been transported here, to Taysha's room, where the rosary's duplicate was.

How long did that interval last?

And Taysha, in Allegra's body, had been touching that faucet, and she was gripping my hand when this transition happened—so I was dragged here along with her. How long will *this* interval last? I don't have the slide rule anymore, I can't open another trap-door.

With an faint click, the light in the kitchen came on, throwing a fan of illumination out across the car and the driveway. Cobb and Allegra crouched against the wall below the window, but Taysha stepped out and leaned against the car, facing the window.

Then she was partially in shadow, and Armand Vitrielli's well-remembered voice spoke from in the kitchen.

"Taysh!" he said. "Where the hell have you been? Was there any mail?"

Pressed against the cold stucco wall, Cobb could feel Allegra's shoulders silently shaking; and he was remembering all the other times he'd heard Vitrielli's voice, laughing delightedly at some joke or pun or clever point of logic, and remembering too the agonized, attenuated voice of the ghost he had uprooted from its rightful rest. He and Allegra both huddled lower.

"Sorry, Dad," said Taysha. "Those dogs from over on Porter were in the yard again, and I was chasing them and then trying to find how they got in." She shrugged. "And no mail."

"Well, come back inside," said Vitrielli. "It's cold out there."

"In a minute, there's just one more section of fence I want to check for holes."

Cobb heard the old man sigh and say, "Well be quick, honey."

Then Cobb felt Allegra tense beside him. She opened her mouth, and before Cobb could stop her she called, "I'm sorry, Dad!"

Taysha gave her double a startled look, and Cobb just closed his eyes.

But Vitrielli's receding voice only said, "S'okay, just don't dawdle." The kitchen light went out, and the sound of his footsteps diminished away down the hall.

Cobb exhaled and tried to relax his tensed muscles.

"Allegra," he said. She pushed him away, sobbing audibly now, and he shook her shoulder. "Listen to me," he hissed, "this unstable interval is about to end, and you need to be holding something metal that you've handled in both worlds! And I need to be touching you when it happens. Think— what is there like that?" She just buried her face in her hands, and he went on harshly, "You want to get back to Lucy, right?"

He stood up and reached a hand down to her.

She waved it away, and then slowly got to her feet. "Hearing his voice again," she whispered. "He said *That's okay,* didn't he? At least." Then she shook her head and blinked at Cobb. "What? Metal? The rosary—"

"It's *used up,*" he said impatiently, "and so's the faucet out back that drew Taysha and I here, they're spent capacitors." He was agonizingly aware of seconds passing, and he resisted the impulse to shake her. "Something else."

"Think about *this*," Taysha said to her; "not," she added with a nod toward the house, "him."

Allegra had stepped out past the front bumper of the car, peering around the yard anxiously. "But there's nothing here that I have there...our wagon's long gone, and the swingset..." She turned to Taysha. "Wait, do you still have our woven leather belt? It has a metal buckle—"

A gust of cold air swept up the driveway, and Cobb jumped, for the old Buick's engine seemed to have started; a moment later he realized that the sound was much quieter than the engine—the car was simply vibrating all over.

Even as a rapid clicking started up in the air, he thought: This car is a link between both worlds, and I must have touched just about every corner of it, in the other world. Lots of my aura signature in it. If I put my hand on it now, it would take me back there. But I should be touching Allegra—

Allegra was standing six feet away, still looking questioningly at Taysha.

How long had Armand Vitrielli had the car? Cobb hesitated only an agonized fraction of a second.

He lunged forward, caught Allegra around the waist and then spun, flinging her at the front end of the old Buick. An apology was already rising in his throat.

She thumped against the hood and rebounded—into nowhere in this world. A brief whirlwind spun where she had been standing, and then he and Taysha were alone with the car in the dark driveway.

III

Cobb's heart was thudding in his chest, and he made his way unsteadily back to the wall by the kitchen window and leaned against it, closing his eyes.

He opened them again when he felt Taysha's hand on his shoulder.

"Do you still have your slide rule thing?" she asked.

"No. I dropped it when you grabbed my hand, back by the faucet. Just as we jumped."

"Oh. Sorry."

He shook his head. The breeze had died, and his damp face just felt hot.

"You could have gone," said Taysha, "instead of her. Right?"

"Yes." He sighed deeply. "I could have gone back *with* her," he said, "if she'd been standing closer to the car. In that moment." He paused, afraid his voice would catch if he said anything more. He took another deep breath and let it out, and said, carefully, "I guessed your father owned the car before you met this Gorba—so she'd probably have had a lot of physical contact with it back then, imprinted a lot of aura signature: opening the doors, the trunk, maybe driving it. It'd link her to the car here and there. But I couldn't be sure."

She squeezed his shoulder and then dropped her hand. "But you took the chance, to send her home. Yes, I've been driving that car since I was sixteen."

"Good. I guess."

"I'm sorry I didn't think of the car. We were thinking of smaller stuff—rosaries, faucets, belts."

He could only wave dismissively.

She shifted on her feet, glancing at the Buick and away. "So Allegra—the other me—is back by the car now, in that empty lot?"

"Somewhere near it. Probably sitting down. I threw her against the hood pretty hard."

"She's back with Lucy, in her own world. Is it—you know—all over now?"

"Without the slide rule, yes, I'm afraid it is. And I'm here."

Taysha stretched, then shivered and crossed her arms. "You marooned yourself here, so that the other me could be back with her daughter, in her life. Her daughter—" She smiled crookedly, "I want to say *our* daughter—isn't deprived of her mother."

"I thought I had to. The whole thing was my fault. Blaine and Ainsworth wouldn't have been able to do it on their own." He yawned so widely that a couple of tears spilled down his cheeks. "I hope she knows how to wedge branches under the tires, so she can back out of that lot. I left the key in the ignition."

"I think it was their fault—Blaine and Ainsworth. I'll tell my dad about them."

Cobb let himself slide down the wall until he was sitting on the cement. "Good idea. But I helped, crucially. I even knew it was wrong."

She sat down near him, and for several seconds neither of them spoke.

"You've got cigarettes," she said finally. "Bum one?"

Cobb touched his shirt pocket, and was remotely surprised to find that his pack of Camels was still there. "Sure."

He straightened one leg to get his lighter out; his hands were shaking, and she took it from him and lit a cigarette for him and one for herself.

Taysha handed the lighter back. "That Lucy kid seemed nice."

"Did she? I guess." He took a deep drag on his cigarette. "There's probably a *me,* somewhere, in this world. Not working for your dad at Cal State, I gather." He exhaled and shook his head. "Doing something worthwhile, do you suppose?"

She nodded thoughtfully. "Well, I'm naturally partial."

"Oh?"

She grinned. "To *Lucy,* I mean. No, if you worked there I'd have met you. I...well, I wouldn't have such a terrible opinion of Dad's colleagues."

He pushed aside thoughts of Googling "Clive Cobb"—and of his Visa card being no good here, and his apartment doubtless being occupied by someone else—and he patted her hand.

"Thanks," he said, then awkwardly moved his hand away. He cleared his throat. "I wonder what other thing I might have done, here, in these—twelve, is it?—years.

What I always *wanted* to do was write kids' books, young adult stuff."

"Maybe he has, this different you. Maybe they're big movies now, like *The Hunger Games.*"

"What," he said, "that Kafka story?"

"No, Suzanne Collins. *The Hunger Games?* Three or four movies? You know, with Jennifer Lawrence?"

He shrugged. "Rings no bells."

She cocked her head. "You do watch movies?"

"Sure, I just don't recall those. Jennifer somebody? I suppose his fingerprints would be the same as mine. If I kill myself, he'll be surprised to hear that his dead body's been found somewhere."

She took a last drag on her cigarette and flicked it away. "You're not going to kill yourself, Clive. Come on, get up. We should go talk to my dad."

She got to her feet and extended her hand down to him. He tossed his own cigarette and took her hand as he stood up.

"We can go in through the kitchen," Taysha said. "His study is down the hall."

He was about to say that he knew the way, but she was still holding his hand, leading him as she pulled open the kitchen door and stepped inside. Together they walked past a newer refrigerator than the one he remembered, and down a hall that didn't have boxes of books shoved up against the walls on both sides. The air was fresher than it had been when he had visited this house in his own world, though he still caught the rich smell of Latakia tobacco.

The door to the study was closed, and the strains of Tchaikovsky's Violin Concerto cut off when Taysha let go of Cobb's hand and knocked. A moment later she pushed the door open.

"Look what I found, Dad," she said, waving Cobb in. "Can I keep him?"

Vitrielli's study appeared to be the same as it was in Cobb's memory—Doré and Piranesi prints above a worn couch, floor-to-ceiling bookshelves on two walls, and a cabinet below a window that he knew was dark even in daytime because of a curtain of lantana branches growing outside. On an old carpet in the center of the room stood a wide, ornate old mahogany table, flanked by two leather armchairs. Tan-shaded lamps stood in two corners, but the face of the old man seated at the desk was lit by a computer monitor.

Now it was Cobb's experiences in the last couple of months that seemed to have happened in a world where he didn't belong. Here was his friend again, and in this moment the remembered funeral had no more relevance than a fleeting dream. The very familiarity of the room was reassuring, and Cobb felt the muscles of his shoulders begin to relax.

Armand Vitrielli took a pipe from his mouth and laid in carefully in a brass ashtray. "Where," he asked, "did you find him?"

"You'll be interested," said Taysha, settling herself on the couch. She looked up at Cobb and patted the cushion beside her.

"I don't mean to impose," said Cobb as he slowly sat down, "but I believe you keep glasses and a bottle of bourbon in the cabinet behind you. Could you spare an inch or two for a trans-reality vagrant?"

Vitrielli's white eyebrows were raised, but after a moment he turned to the cabinet and said, "Tell me about this, Taysha."

III

What with increasingly intent questions from the old man, and Taysha and Cobb interrupting each other as they took turns telling the story, an hour had passed by the time Vitrielli sat back and picked up his pipe again.

He pushed a pipe cleaner through it, pulled it out and dropped it into a wastepaper basket, then thoughtfully struck a wooden match and re-lit the pipe. As smoke curled toward the ceiling, he squinted at Taysha.

"You *married* that Lou Gorba fellow?"

"A different me, in a different world."

"Fair enough." Vitrielli's head bobbed gently as he looked around the room. "I should quarantine this house, I suppose." He tamped the tobacco in his pipe and eyed Cobb over the top of it. "Your Blaine and Ainsworth," he said, puffing, "should have quarantined Taysha. God knows what pathogens might be unique to one world or the other. Oh well—at least you weren't antimatter." He waved at the smoke overhead and said, "You've got cigarettes; feel free."

"Thanks." Cobb fetched out his somewhat battered pack of Camels and his lighter.

Vitrielli went on, "And I—*killed* myself! That's distressing." With his free hand he lifted the glass in front of him and took a sip. "Ainsworth and Blaine may be substantially different people here than they evidently are where you come from, sir— threaten my daughter!—but the similarities are enough that I'm afraid I'll have to look into their projects more closely, and at the very least begin edging them aside."

In the other world, Vitrielli had always called him Clive. Cobb glanced away, and saw that Taysha was eyeing the pack of cigarettes, and he held it toward her so that she could pinch one out.

"I find I'm embarrassed," mused Vitrielli, "that you two saw my poor ghost."

"My fault," said Cobb. "I'm very sorry."

"Interesting bit of data, though." Vitrielli pushed his chair back and stood up. "It's true," he said, looking over their heads at the framed prints on the wall, "that I've been studying transmigration of souls, and I think transfer of a mind to a different body is achievable." He paused to give them a surprised look. "Well, you two have seen it happen, haven't you? Luckily I have not told anyone—in this world!—about that possibility. Technomancy today is as discreditable as mesmerism was in the 18th century—"

Cobb had heard him say this before, and unthinkingly finished Vitrielli's sentence: "—but Einstein went to séances, and the physicists at CERN make offerings to a statue of Shiva."

Vitrielli paused with his mouth still open, then closed it and gave Cobb a baffled smile. "Yes. Precisely. I think we *have* talked before, in your world."

"And I'm in this one now," said Cobb; "and I'm entirely extra." He lifted his glass and took a gulp of the bourbon. "Worse than no place for me—there *is* a place for me, but somebody's already in it. Probably. I'll find out, whenever I might get fingerprinted."

Vitrielli looked at him curiously. "If you choose to stay."

"I don't see how I can get back to where I came from."

"Oh, that." Vitrielli sat down at the desk and opened a drawer. He lifted out a wooden box Cobb had seen before, and when he opened it Cobb saw, in its velvet-lined interior, a duplicate of the slide rule he had dropped by the backyard faucet in the other world. "And you must very often have touched the doorknob of my office at the Consciousness Research Department in McCarthy Hall, I imagine? In your world?"

"Yes," said Cobb. "Uh...yes."

"We'd have to remove the doorknob," said Vitrielli, "in order for me to be able to walk around it, but," he waved the slide rule, "I do know how this thing works."

To his surprise, Cobb only felt deflated. Perhaps he faced no overwhelming challenge after all—just the prospect of finding a new position at another college somewhere. He was looking into the familiar eyes of Vitrielli across the desk, but smoke from Taysha's newly lit cigarette drifted into his vision from beside him, and he turned his head to look at her. I'd never see Vitrielli— or Taysha!—again, he thought; never again visit this house.

"But" he objected, without looking away from her, "would I *last,* there, stay there?"

He heard Vitrielli say, "Assuming you don't find the other slide rule and go playing with it—yes."

Cobb shifted sideways on the couch, and then found that he could think of nothing to say.

Taysha smiled sadly and touched his chest with her free hand. "I guess I don't get to keep you after all?"

Vitrielli rapped out his pipe in the ashtray. "Blaine said they were in correspondence with...*allied institutions?* And had applied for grants? And Ainsworth said something about 'housing for subjects.'" He gave Cobb a direct look. "And that little girl, Lucy, needs to find an incriminating tape. I know where I'd have hidden it, in that car—in the slot above the diagnostic link connector, under the dashboard. Any service technician would find it in a moment, but I don't think Lucy or...her mother, would poke their fingers in there. Unless somebody advised them to." He sat back. "Of course it's not my world."

For several seconds no one spoke.

"That's all true," said Cobb. "I guess it was never really—yes, you're right. Of course."

Taysha nodded and looked down at her hands. "Write children's books," she said.

Cobb managed a smile. "Blaine said I should take up fiction writing."

"Well!" said Vitrielli. "I can't get into the building until eight tomorrow morning, so..." He stepped to the window and crouched to open the cabinet below it. Cobb guessed that he was going to fetch out the Panasonic tape recorder he kept there for making notes to himself—and sometimes perhaps taping telephone calls. "We can spend the night comparing worlds."

"Clive never heard of *The Hunger Games,* or Jennifer Lawrence," said Taysha, "though he keeps up with movies."

"Excellent start," said Vitrielli, straightening up with the recorder and crossing to the desk. "If I dared, I'd give you a DVD of it to take back with you." He plugged the recorder's extension into a wall socket, then sat down and pushed two buttons on the machine. "Do you keep up with politics, sir?"

"Do call me Clive."

"Clive," said Vitrielli, pointing at the recorder, "the wheels are turning."

"Right. Well, let's see..."

As Cobb began trying to sketch in his recollections of the history of the last twelve years, Taysha yawned and shifted on the couch, leaning her head on his shoulder.

Vitrielli soon had to open a fresh package of tape cassettes.

By dawn, Cobb and the old man had recounted everything they could manage to recall about politics, science, movies, books, earthquakes, and even popular songs and ethnic restaurants. There were few discrepancies, and those mostly in areas where one of them would logically be ignorant, though Vitrielli had not heard of the discovery of all forty-two film reels of Von Stroheim's 1924 movie *Greed*, and Cobb was delighted to learn that in this world Elon Musk had sent a Tesla automobile into perpetual orbit around the earth.

Taysha had spent most of the time asleep on Cobb's shoulder, but woke at a scratching at the door. She sat up and blinked blearily around for several seconds, then visibly recalled the circumstances. "Do they," she said to her father, then paused to yawn; "have orbital colonies?" When he smiled tiredly and shook his head, she stood up and stretched. "The cats want breakfast. Eggs and bacon okay for the rest of us?"

III

Vitrielli's Buick was blowing white smoke across the driveway. Cobb was sitting on the passenger seat with the door open and his feet on the pavement as he held a cup of coffee in both hands. Taysha stood beside the car, leaning over him with one hand braced on the doorframe. She had said that she would just as soon "make a cat's goodbye," and not come along to the university and see Cobb disappear.

Cobb listened to the engine. "You want to get a new EGR valve," he said over his shoulder.

"Noted," said Vitrielli, fluttering the gas pedal. "But it'll be warm enough to shift into gear soon."

"I'll remember it," said Taysha.

"You'll find that slide rule," said Vitrielli, "and—"

"I'll find it and destroy it, don't worry," said Cobb.

"And Clive," Vitrielli went on, "you will remember to tell Allegra there's no hard feelings, right? That's as important as any of the rest of it, to me. Tell her I always loved her, in every world."

Taysha bent down to peer past Cobb at her father. "We all love every one of you too, Dad." She looked sideways at Cobb. "You could get to know her."

Cobb thought of several pointless things he could say, then contented himself with, "Not the same."

Vitrielli was now gunning the engine to keep the car from stalling. "I'd have liked to meet my granddaughter," he remarked.

Taysha avoided Cobb's eye as she straightened up.

"Still," she said, "I think I might look for Clive Cobb, here. He can't be too different."

"Tell him...tell him to make up for my shortcomings."

"That wouldn't take too much work." She leaned in and kissed him, then stood back and waved, for her father had clanked the car into reverse.